Charlie's Birthday Present

Story and pictures by BERNICE MYERS

SCHOLASTIC BOOK SERVICES
NEW YORK · TORONTO · LONDON · AUCKLAND · SYDNEY · TOKYO

To David and Dara

ISBN: 0-590-31992-2

12 11 10 9 8 7 6 5 4 3 2 1   3   1 2 3 4 5 6/8
                                    Printed in the U.S.A.   07

Charlie
woke up early
one spring morning.
It was his birthday.
He saw a present
at the foot of
his bed.

"It could be a robot!
Or maybe a giant rabbit?"

Charlie
pulled the ribbon
and tore off the paper.

"A tree?

For my birthday?"

Charlie
looked around.
Maybe there was
another present, too.

"I always get a
toy
on my birthday,"
he said.

"Well,"
his father said,
"this year
your mother and I
thought that
a tree
would be just the thing.
There are no wheels
to come off,
no batteries to die,
no switch to break."

"But I can't have
any fun
with a tree."

"How do you know?"
his mother said.

Charlie
took his tree
outside
and dug a hole.

When it was deep enough,
he pushed the tree
into the hole.
Then he filled the hole
with dirt
and watered it.

"So far,
you're not much fun,"
Charlie said.

Leaves
began to grow
on Charlie's tree.
At Easter time
he hid some
eggs
in its branches.

In summer
he played hide and seek
with his friends.

In the fall
Charlie
raked the leaves
that fell from
his tree.

And in winter
he decorated
the branches.

"You are sort of fun,"
Charlie said,
"...for a tree."

When spring came again,
so did Charlie's birthday.
Charlie woke up early.
He saw a present
on his bed.

"Trains!
I'm sure it's trains!
Or maybe
it's a pet snake."

Charlie
pulled the ribbon
and tore off the paper.

So Charlie

took his hose

and watered his tree...

. . . thoroughly.

The next year
on his birthday,
Charlie
found a present
on his bed.

"A basketball!
Or maybe a
football helmet!"

"A wooden house?

For my birthday?"

"That's right,"
said his mother.
"It's a bird house.
Put some
bird seed inside
and hang it on
your tree.
Then see what happens."

At first
nothing happened.
Then a robin flew inside.
Then another.
Soon there were eggs.

All through the
spring and summer,
the robin family
lived in Charlie's bird house
on Charlie's tree.

When winter came,
the birds left.
"Don't worry, Charlie.
They'll be back
next spring,"
his father said.

The robins
did come back.
They came back
on Charlie's birthday!

When Charlie
woke up
he saw a
tremendous present
on his bed.

"It's a red bicycle!
Or maybe a racing car!"

Charlie
pulled the ribbon
and tore off the paper.

"A ladder?

For my birthday?"

"You'll need it
when you
pick the cherries
on your tree
this summer."

"It's a cherry tree,"
Charlie told his friends.
"But we have to
wait a while
for the cherries."

Each day
his friends came
and asked,

"Are there any cherries yet?"

"Are the cherries ripe yet?"

"I don't see any cherries."

"Yum."

At last
there were cherries—
big and red.

"We can
pick them now,"
Charlie said.

"Can I try your ladder?"

"Charlie's my best friend."

"Yum."

There were
enough cherries
for everyone.

"Hurray for Charlie,"
his friends said.

"Hurray for
my tree,"
said Charlie.